Superbot: Toad and the Goo Extractor
is a DAVID FICKLING BOOK

First published in Great Britain in 2016 by
David Fickling Books,
31 Beaumont Street,
Oxford, OX1 2NP

Text and illustrations © Nick Ward, 2016

978-1-910200-31-5

1 3 5 7 9 10 8 6 4 2

David Fickling Books supports the
Forest Stewardship Council® (FSC)®,
the leading international
forest certification organisation.
All our titles that are printed on
Greenpeace-approved FSC-certified
paper carry the FSC logo.

MIX
Paper from
responsible sources
FSC
www.fsc.org   FSC® C104723

DAVID FICKLING BOOKS Reg. No. 8340307
A CIP catalogue record for this book is available from the British Library

Printed and bound in China by Toppan Leefung.

dfbees

SUPERBOT

TOAD AND THE GOO EXTRACTOR

NICK WARD

David Fickling Books

CHAPTER 1
Calling BOT!

Bot's house

Radar scanner

Bot the Super Robot lives with his inventor, Mrs Brightspark, in their secret headquarters on top of a very tall skyscraper.

3

← Mrs Brightspark!

"There is naughtiness all around us," Mrs Brightspark says, so she's fitted Bot with lots of useful gadgets.

He can swim as fast as a speedboat and walk up walls with his super-suction feet.

He can see in the dark and hear a mouse squeak on the moon!

Cheese!

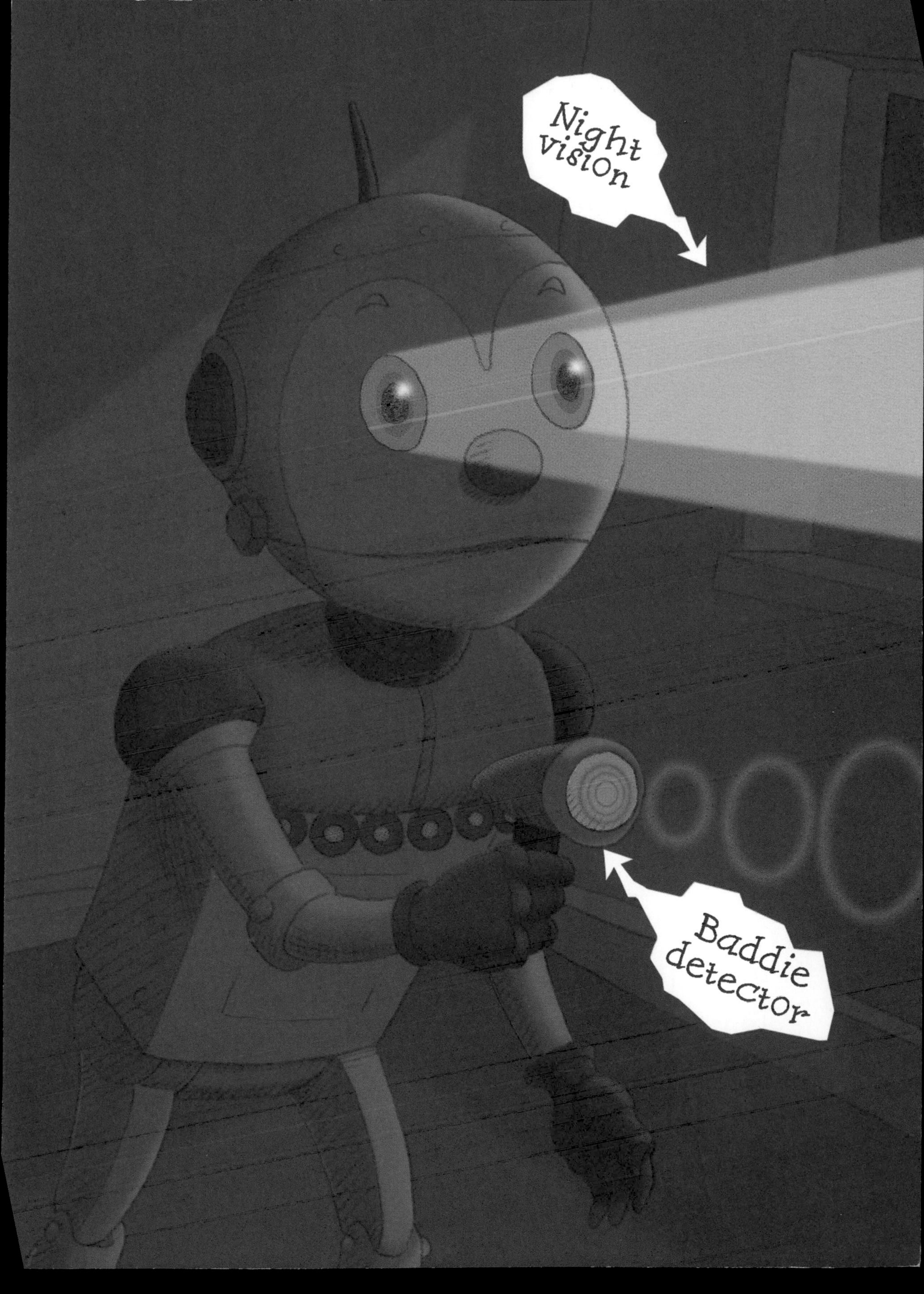
Night vision
Baddie detector

One day Bot's Trouble Tracking
System started to beep.

"Calling Bot. SOS!" crackled the
loud speaker. "Terrible Toad is causing
mayhem!"

"Oh no! *Fizz pop*," said Bot. "Terrible
Toad is always being naughty."

6

"Not that toad again," gasped Mrs
Brightspark, hurrying into Bot's room.

She was in the middle of making
strawberry jam, and had a big red blob
of it on her nose. "You'd better hurry.
But make sure you're home before
teatime."

Bot ran down the garden path, fired up his rocket pack and leaped from the edge of the skyscraper. *Whoosh!* He roared across the sky. "Up and away. Bot to the rescue!"

Rooftop garden of Bot H.Q.

WHOOSH!

Bot could tell something was
wrong because there were no children
playing in the streets below. He
landed in a playground to look for
clues. There were footballs and
skipping ropes and skateboards
lying about, but all the children had
disappeared. It was spooky!

Suddenly, Bot's hypersensitive ears heard a strange gurgling noise.

"*Fizz, pop!* Sounds like trouble," said Bot. He took off, flying high over the rooftops. In the distance he spotted a commotion.

"It's Toad!" said Bot, and shot off after him with rockets blasting.

GURGLE, SHLUP!

CHAPTER 2

The Terrible Toad!

Squeak, squeak!

Tom and his friends were running helter-skelter down the street. Above them, Terrible Toad was pedalling an amazing flying bike.

On the back it looked like there was a big vacuum cleaner.

"Go away, Toad," shouted Tom.

"*Ribbit*, you go away!" croaked Terrible Toad, pointing the vacuum cleaner's hosepipe at him. SHLUP! the boy was sucked inside.

"*Fizz, pop!* Let Tom go, you fiendish frog," said Bot, making sure he kept out of reach of the noisy machine.

"*Boip!* Go and oil yourself, Bot,"
belched Toad. He chased after the
other children, and . . .

SHLUP!

SHLUP!

WHOOSH!

PUFF!

Toad hoovered up
Lucy, then Daisy and
Ben and zoomed
off towards a sinister
black building.

"*Ribbit, ribbit,*"
sniggered Toad,
pedalling into his lair
and slamming the door
behind him.

Bot flew to a tall
chimney on top of the
building and dived
inside.

He emerged in a cloud of soot inside
Terrible Toad's den.

Toad was emptying the children one
by one into an awful spinning
machine!

"*Ribbit, ribbit,*" chuckled Toad.

CHAPTER 3

The Goo Extractor!

errible Toad landed next to a control panel and pulled a lever. The spinning machine started to turn faster and faster and the children began to shriek.

"*Fzzz!* Bot to the rescue!" announced
Bot, rocketing into the air. Toad
burped and pressed a button.
A chain dropped from the ceiling.
On the end were lots of curved metal
bars that snapped shut
around Bot. He was
trapped!

"Let me go, *fizz pop!*" he demanded. "What are you doing to those children, you terrible toad?"

"Calm down, Bot. I'm only extracting their juice for my flypapers," said Toad, with a satisfied smile.

Bzzz!

Bzzz!

Bzzz!

Bzzz!

Bzzz!

"Extracting their juice?" Bot cried, shaking the bars of his cage.

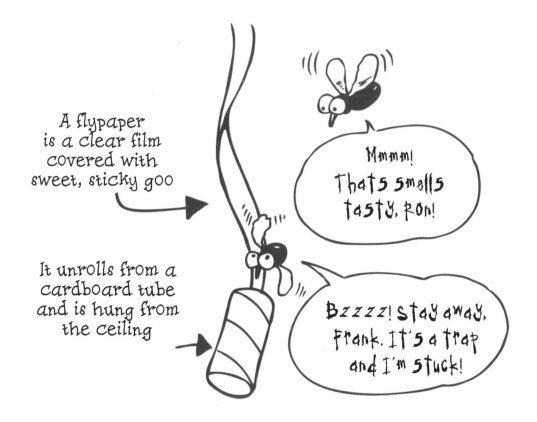

"I catch flies for my supper on sticky flypapers, but I've run out of special glue to coat them with," said Toad.

"Kiddies eat so many sweets and drink so much sugary pop, they are full of stickiness. A quick spin in my goo extractor, and I've got all the syrupy glue I need."

"You terrible, terrible toad," fizzed Bot.

"It doesn't hurt 'em," croaked Toad, pulling the lever and increasing the speed of the spinner even more. "It just shrinks them a bit."

Ribbit, ribbit, ribbit!

Bot took the laser torch from his tummy hatch and began to burn through the bars of the cage with its invisible beam.

With a sudden crash, the bars of the cage fell to the ground. Bot flew out with his zapper gun at the ready.

He blasted the stop button on the spinning machine and it juddered to a halt.

A door in the spinner sprang open and a pile of mini children tumbled out.

"Oh no. Look what he's done to us!" squeaked a tiny Tom.

"I'm no bigger than a doll!" said a little Lucy.

"You interfering android!" burped Toad, and he leaped on his bike and took off.

As he raced towards Bot he grabbed
the tube of his vacuum cleaner and
turned its switch to "BLOW".

CHAPTER 4

Bye Bye, Toad!

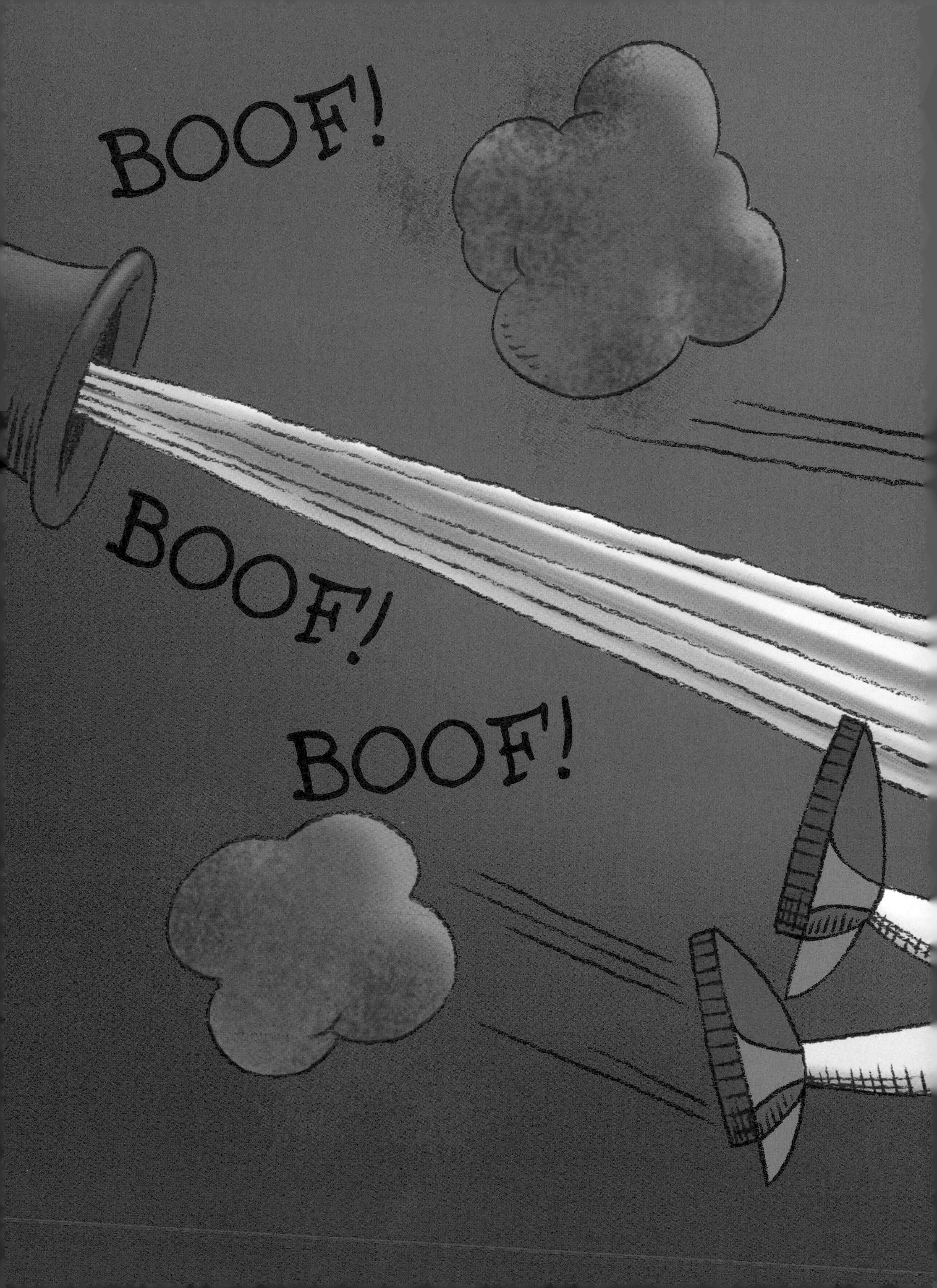
BOOF!
BOOF!
BOOF!

Balls of dust shot from the tube and exploded in little clouds all around Bot. *Boof!* One hit him in the tummy and he crashed to the ground.

Emergency! Emergency!

"Got you!" grinned Terrible Toad as he hovered on his bike above Bot. He turned his vacuum machine back to "SUCK".

But as he pointed the tube at the little robot, Toad's long scarf got dragged inside and started to pull him in after it!

Gurgle!
Gurgle!

"Help!" croaked Terrible Toad as first his head, his round body and then his big boots disappeared up the tube with a loud gurgling noise.

"*Fizz, pop!* So long, Terrible Toad," chuckled Bot, and ran across to the children.

"What are we going to do?" asked a weeny Wendy.

"Don't worry, I have a plan," said Bot, but just then a loud grinding noise made him look up.

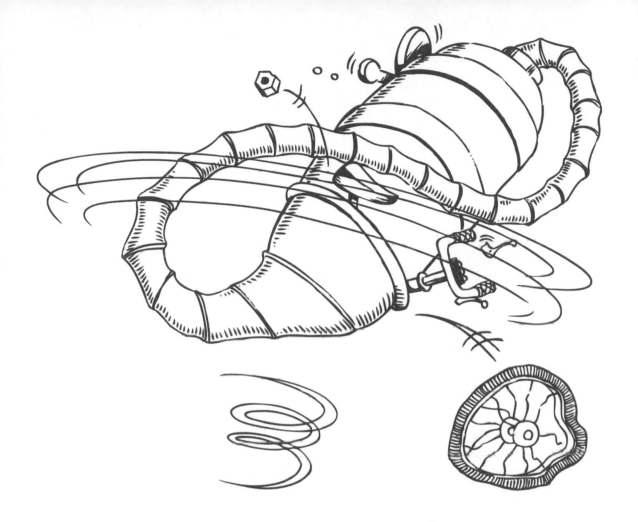

Uh, oh! The vacuum cleaner on the
back of Toad's bike was getting sucked
into its own hosepipe. The motor
started to whine and shake, and then
the whole thing began to spin like a
top. As the last bit disappeared up the
hosepipe . . . **BOOM!**

There was a
mighty explosion
of dust
that filled
the room.

When it cleared, all that was left was
a forlorn, tiny and very grubby toad
sitting on the ground. While Toad was
still in a daze, Bot picked him up and
popped him in an empty jam jar.

"Where am I?" croaked Toad, peering through the glass sides. "*Buuurp!*"

"You're coming with us," Bot told him. "Come on, everyone. I know someone who will be able to help."

CHAPTER 5

A Special Tea

"You did very well, Bot," said Mrs Brightspark when he'd finished telling his story. "Now, lay the table while I get Lucy and her friends one of my special teas."

Soon the table was groaning under the weight of jam sponges, sticky buns and sweeties. "Tuck in, kids," said Mrs Brightspark, and they did!

"Look at me," cried Lucy. As she munched a big slice of cake, she started to grow and grow. So did her friends, and soon they were all back to their proper size.

Anti-gravity lift

Bot's house

"I think you're ready to go home, now," said Mrs Brightspark.

"Bye, Bot. Bye, Mrs Brightspark," they called as they raced happily out of the house and took the anti-gravity lift all the way down to the bottom of the skyscraper.

"*Bzzz*, what about Terrible Toad?" Bot whispered. "Can you do anything for him?"

"Of course," said Mrs Brightspark, crossing her arms and looking at the hapless toad.

Yes, Mrs Brightspark had let Terrible Toad have some tea, and now he was back to his normal size too!

"If you promise to be a good toad," she said, sternly, "I will give you some jars of my extra sticky jam to put on your flypapers."

"Oh, I promise. I do, I do, *burp*," said Toad. "Pardon." He looked so earnest, Mrs Brightspark loaded him up with jars of extra sticky jam.

"Right," she said opening the front door. "I don't want to hear about any more naughtiness. Off you go."

"Yes, Mrs Brightspark. *Burp!*" said Toad and shuffled hurriedly away.

CHAPTER 6

Emergency!

B ot and Mrs Brightspark sat at
their kitchen table being very
busy. Mrs Brightspark was working
on some new inventions and Bot was
doing a drawing of Terrible Toad.

"*Fizz, pop!* Do you think Terrible Toad will be good from now on?" he asked.

There is naughtiness all around us!

"Who knows? There is naughtiness all around us!" said Mrs Brightspark. "That's why I invented you. A super robot that tracks down baddies everywhere."

Just then the Trouble Tracking System in Bot's bedroom started to beep. "*Calling Bot. SOS!*"

"*Fzzz!* Oh no," he said, running into his room and checking the screen. "The Burglar Brothers have ransacked the toyshop!"

S.O.S!

Bot's Room

"Oh dear, and just before Christmas, too," said Mrs Brightspark. "You'd better hurry, Bot. But make sure you're home in time for refuelling."

As he ran across the skyscraper's
roof, Bot pressed a button and the
rocket pack unfolded on his back.
With a burst of flame it roared
into life and Bot leaped from the
edge of the building and zoomed
across the sky.

Bruto the Bad is on the rampage,
stealing toys and crunching
them up.
Can Bot stop his naughtiness?

Look out for another exciting instalment of

SUPERBOT